MOTHER GOOSE MONSTERS®
in
MONSTER TALES

Written by **Alfa-Betty Olsen and Marshall Efron**

Illustrated by **Richard Walz**

This book is dedicated to Molly O'Neil—A-B.O. and M.E.
For Mary—R.N.W.

It was a dark and stormy night. Inside Monster Goose's house all the little Monsters were cozy and warm.

"Tonight we're going to tell spooky fairy tales around the boiling stew pot," said Monster Goose.

"Oh, goody," said Zazu and clapped her hands. Outside the thunder clapped, too. Moe, Hexter, and Zack clutched each other. Goria clutched her pet cat, Google, who was just as big as she was.

"I know a true spooky story," said Goria. "This happened to a friend of mine, a little troll girl who was called Little Red Baseball Cap because she always wore a big red baseball cap."

Goria's Story

One day Little Red Baseball Cap had to bring a basket of goodies to her grandmother's house in the deep, dark forest. In the basket there were pickled frogs' eggs, toadstool salad, rotten log biscuits, and a bottle of sweetened snail slime. "Don't dillydally," said her mother. "And don't talk to any three-eyed, long-snouted beasts with sharp pointy teeth."

"I promise," said Little Red Baseball Cap.

Little Red Baseball Cap set out. As soon as she entered the forest, she met a beast named Bill. He had three eyes, a long snout, and sharp pointy teeth.

"Where are you going?" asked Bill the Beast.

"To my grandmother's house on Duck Feather Lane," said Little Red Baseball Cap, dillydallying.

"I know a shortcut," said Bill the Beast. "You go this way and that way. And then around and back and then turn and go forward and you can't miss it."

"Thank you," said Little Red Baseball Cap.

She went this way and that way. And then around and back and then she turned and went forward. Bill the Beast went straight to Grandmother's house intending to eat Grandmother.

But Grandmother saw the beast and ran away before he could eat her. So the beast decided to eat Little Red Baseball Cap instead.

Bill the Beast put on Grandmother's nightcap, got into her bed, and waited for Little Red Baseball Cap.

As soon as Little Red Baseball Cap walked into Grandmother's house, she suspected that all was not right.

"You're not my grandmother," she said to the beast. "You have three eyes."

"The better to see you with, my dear," said the beast.

"You're not my grandmother, you have a big snout," said Little Red Baseball Cap.

"The better to snort at you, my dear," said the beast, snorting.

"You're not my grandmother, you have big sharp teeth," said Little Red Baseball Cap.

"The better to gobble you up, my dear," said the beast, jumping out of the bed.

"Oh, no, you don't," said Little Red Baseball Cap. "I have a basket of goodies. Eat that."

Bill the Beast ate all the pickled frogs' eggs, the toadstool salad, the rotten log biscuits, and the whole bottle of sweetened snail slime.

"Yum, yum," he said. "Thank you. That was good. I'll be on my way now." And the beast went home.

As soon as he was gone, Little Red Baseball Cap's grandmother came out of the cupboard where she had been hiding.

"What are we going to do?" said Little Red Baseball Cap. "I gave all our food to the beast and now we have none."

"We'll just have to go to a baseball game and eat peanuts and popcorn instead," said Grandmother. And they did!

"That was a good spooky story, Goria," said Monster Goose.

"I've got goose bumps," said Moe.

"I'm glad to hear it," said Monster Goose. "Would you like to tell a story now?"

"Oh, yes," said Moe. "I'd love to tell a story now. Hang on to your shivers, here it comes."

Moe's Story

Once upon a spooky time there were three little blue goblins named Joe, Flo, and Arnold. They lived beside a graveyard in three little houses. Joe lived in a house made of spiderwebs. Flo lived in a house made of dead leaves. Arnold lived in a house made of old tombstones. Every night they danced together in the moonlight.

One hot day a big, bad dust devil came by and knocked on Joe's door. "Little goblin, little goblin, let me in," he said.

Joe grew blue goose bumps. "Not by the bumps on my pretty blue skin," he said.

"Then I'll spin and I'll twirl and I'll blow your house in," said the dust devil. He spun and twirled and the house of spiderwebs blew away.

"Eeeeek," said Joe as he ran to his sister Flo's house.

The dust devil followed him down the road and knocked
on Flo's door.

"Little goblin, little goblin, let me in," he shouted.

Flo's blood ran so cold, she sweat ice cubes. "Not by the
bumps on my pretty blue skin," she said.

"Then I'll spin and I'll twirl and I'll blow your house in," said
the dust devil. And he spun and twirled and blew the house of
dead leaves away.

"Eeeeek," said Flo as she and Joe ran to their brother
Arnold's house.

The dust devil followed them down the road and knocked on Arnold's door. "Little goblin, little goblin, let me in," he shouted.

Arnold giggled a goblin guffaw. "Not by the bumps on my pretty blue skin."

"Then I'll spin and I'll twirl and I'll blow your house in," said the dust devil.

"My house is made of tombstones. You can't blow it in,"
said Arnold.

"Watch this," said the dust devil, and he spun and twirled, but
the house wouldn't fall down. This made the dust devil so mad
that he spun and twirled again, but still the house wouldn't fall
down.

"I'll get you yet," said the dust devil. He climbed up onto the roof, leapt to the top of the chimney, put his right foot in and his left foot in, slid straight down, and the dust devil was in the little tombstone house! The goblins ran into the closet and locked the door behind them.

"Come out," yelled the dust devil. "Come out!"

Now everybody knows that if you yell "Come out" near a graveyard, you are likely to get a response. That's why nobody ever does it.

But the dust devil yelled "Come out" again, and deep in the graveyard, beneath a huge tombstone, a great big zombie heard the dust devil call.

"Nobody's asked me out in ages," said the zombie. She put on her best hat, shuffled over to Arnold's house, and broke down the door.

"Hi, handsome," the zombie said to the dust devil, and she smiled a toothless smile.

The dust devil yelled, "Help, it's a zombie!" and he spun and twirled himself far away.

The three little goblins were free at last. To celebrate, they danced with the zombie in the moonlight.

"And that's the end of my story," said Moe.

"It's your turn, Hexter," said Monster Goose.

Hexter sat up tall and got ready to tell his tale.

"This story is my favorite story," he began. "So listen carefully."

Hexter's Story

Once upon a tiny time a little elf named Jack and his mom lived happily together in Small Valley. They were only 12 inches tall, but they had a regular-sized cow named Andra who gave lots of milk. So Jack and his mom ate milky things: cheese, yogurt, and cream of tomato soup. Even their house was made of cottage cheese. Since they liked milk, they were very happy.

Then a bad thing happened: The dish ran away with the spoon. This caused Andra the cow to jump over the moon. After that she stopped giving milk.

"If we have to count on Andra," said Jack, "we're going to starve."

"We'll have to sell her and get another cow," said his mom.

On his way to the market Jack met a wizard hopping along the path.

"I've always wanted a jumping cow," said the wizard. "I don't have any money, but I can give you these jumping beans. Plant them and you'll get lucky."

Jack thought this was a good trade. So he handed over Andra and went home with the beans.

But Jack's mom was angry. "We can't eat jumping beans," she said and threw the beans out the window. That night for dinner they had to eat part of the chimney. When they looked up they could see the stars through the hole they had made.

The next morning Jack awoke to find that the beans had grown into a huge vine that was so tall, Jack and his mom could not see the top.

"I'm going to climb it," said Jack. "Maybe I'll find luck at the top. While I'm gone, you can eat the roof."

"Hurry," said his mom. "I'm so hungry, I could eat the whole house."

So up Jack climbed. At the top of the vine, Jack found another country and in it he found a house, bigger than any he had ever seen. The door of the house opened and a vicious giant pixie named Mad-Dog stepped out. He kicked the door closed, spat on his cat, ripped a rose from his rosebush, threw it away, and put a thorn in his lapel. Then Mad-Dog went off into the woods behind his house and Jack slipped inside.

The first thing Jack saw was a big duck sitting in the corner tied to a hook.

"Hi, little elf," said the duck. "My name is Lucky Ducky. What's yours, and what brings you here?"

"I was looking for luck," said Jack, who then told Lucky Ducky his sad story.

"You did find luck, you found me," said Lucky Ducky. "That vicious giant pixie, Mad-Dog, is a mean old guy. He washes his face in the frying pan, combs his hair with the leg of a chair, and goes to bed in his underwear. Unhook me and take me away and I will live with you and your mom and give you an egg a week, which from the looks of you, should be plenty."

"It's a deal," said Jack.

Just then he heard the vicious giant pixie Mad-Dog coming back. "What shall I do?" he asked.

"Quick, hide in the oven," said Lucky Ducky, and Jack jumped into the oven and closed the door.

"Fee, fi, fo, fum," said the vicious giant pixie Mad-Dog. "I smell a tiny elf crumb. Where is the little snack hiding?"

"There are no elves around here," said Lucky Ducky. Then she quickly laid an egg.

"Yo, lunch," said the vicious giant pixie Mad-Dog.

When he finished the egg, he sniffed the air again. "Fee, fi, fo, fum," he said. "I smell a tiny elf crumb."

"Now that you mention it twice, so do I," said Lucky Ducky. "He's hiding in the chimney."

The vicious giant pixie Mad-Dog climbed into the chimney. But he was so big, he got stuck.

"Help!" he cried.

"Sit on my back, Jack, and I'll run," said Lucky Ducky.

They were out the door in a flash and well on their way before the vicious giant pixie Mad-Dog wiggled out of the chimney and ran after them.

Lucky Ducky jumped off the edge of the country, flapped her wings, and sailed down to Small Valley with Jack on her back.

The vicious giant pixie Mad-Dog found the jumping bean vine and climbed down and down and down.

Jack's mom ran out of the house with an axe in her hand. "Cut the vine," she hollered.

Jack swung the axe at the vine as hard as he could and the vine fell over. The vicious giant pixie Mad-Dog fell onto the ground so hard, it was the end of him.

Lucky Ducky lived with Jack and his mom, who ate one egg a week. Jack used the eggshells to mend the hole in the roof. One day it rained, filling the crater that Mad-Dog had made when he fell. Soon Lucky Ducky had a nice duck pond.

The stew wasn't quite ready. And the rain was still coming down in buckets. Monster Goose turned to Zack.

"Zack," she said. "You'll have to tell us a story, too."

"I know a good story," said Zack. "Here it is."

Zack's Story

Once upon a haunted time three fire-breathing dragons lived in a house together. There was a big Papa Dragon, a medium-sized Mama Dragon, and a little Baby Dragon.

One day Mama Dragon made oatmeal for their breakfast, but it was too hot for them to eat. Because dragons breathe fire all the time, they need to eat cold food to cool off their tongues. So the three dragons went out for a walk to give the oatmeal plenty of time to get good and cold.

While the dragons were gone, a little witch, who was just learning to ride, flew by on her broomstick. She was quite lost and hungry and she decided to go into the house and find something to eat.

The little witch found the oatmeal in the kitchen and tasted it.

"Umm. Good! Nice and warm," she said and ate it all up. She ate Papa Dragon's big bowl of oatmeal. She ate Mama Dragon's medium-sized bowl of oatmeal. And she ate Baby Dragon's little bowl of oatmeal.

Then she went into the parlor to find a seat and rest. "Oh, goody," she said. "Three chairs to choose from: a big chair, a medium-sized chair, and a little chair."

She sat in the big chair, but it was too hard. She sat in the medium-sized chair, but it was too soft. She sat in the baby chair and it was just right, and she rocked back and forth and back and forth, and then she broke the chair. So she went upstairs to look for a bed.

Upstairs the witch found three beds: a big bed, a medium-sized bed, and a little bed. She lay down in the big bed, but it was too hard. She lay down on the medium-sized bed, but it was too soft. She lay down on the small bed and it was just right, so she fell asleep.

Just then the three dragons came home.

"SOMEONE HAS EATEN ALL MY OATMEAL," said Papa Dragon, and he breathed fire.

"*Someone has eaten all my oatmeal,*" said Mama Dragon, and she breathed fire.

"Someone has eaten all my oatmeal," said Baby Dragon, and he breathed little sparks.

They went into the parlor.

"SOMEONE HAS SAT IN MY CHAIR," said Papa Dragon, and he breathed fire.

"*Someone has sat in my chair,*'" said Mama Dragon, and she breathed fire.

"Someone has sat in my chair and broke it!" said Baby Dragon, and he breathed little sparks.

They went upstairs.

"SOMEONE HAS MUSSED UP MY BED," said Papa Dragon.

"*Someone has mussed up my bed,*" said Mama Dragon.

"Someone has mussed up my bed and is still sleeping in it!" said Baby Dragon.

"GET OUT!" yelled Papa Dragon, and flames shot out of his snout.

"*Get out!*" yelled Mama Dragon, and flames shot out of her snout.

"Get out!" yelled Baby Dragon, and sparks flew from his snout.

The little witch woke up. She had never seen a dragon before and was a little surprised and nervous. "I'm going," she said. "Just don't get so hot under the collar." With that, she ran away.

"**GOOD-BYE!**" yelled the dragons, and their flames burned the house down and they had to go and live in a cave. But that was all right. Dragons like caves better than houses because caves don't burn down.

"Now it's my turn," said Zazu. "My story is the spookiest one of all. Are you ready?"

"We're ready," said Goria, Moe, Zack, and Hexter.

"I'm ready, too," said Monster Goose.

Zazu's Story

Once upon a creepy time a beautiful purple princess with long hairy teeth and short hairy curls lived in a castle on the edge of an enchanted swamp. It was always nighttime and bats, werewolves, vampires, black slithery snakes, and swamp monsters lived there.

One night the king announced it was time for the princess to get married. Three bats, four werewolves, two black slithery snakes, one vampire, one wizard, and a swamp monster asked for her hand.

"They're too spooky," said the princess. "Send them away."

The bats, the werewolves, the snakes, and the vampire went back to their old haunts in a huff. The swamp monster was very disappointed and he crept back to his lagoon to mope in peace.

But the wizard was angry and he cast a spell upon the princess. "You and everyone in the castle will sleep until the sun rises," he said.

That night everybody in the castle went to sleep, but since it was always nighttime in the kingdom, the sun never came up and they never woke up. Years went by, the wizard died of old age, and no one could remove the spell.

One day a handsome purple prince with long, hairy teeth and short hairy curls came riding through the kingdom. The moon was full, werewolves howled, bats flew everywhere, and vampires crept around saying, "Good evening."

All of a sudden a big, slithery snake jumped out of a tree right onto the prince. He squeezed the prince and told him the story of the castle. "That castle is under a spell. Anyone who goes to sleep inside it will never wake up," he hissed. "Go in and take a look."

The prince went inside and saw the sleeping princess. He fell in love with her purple skin, her long hairy teeth, and her short hairy curls. "We are made for each other," he said.

He waited for her to wake up, but she didn't. Before long the prince grew tired. He yawned. His eyes closed. He was falling asleep!

The prince went to the window and cried, "Help me!"

Down in the black lagoon, the swamp monster heard him. He was tall, gooey, very strong, and he had a good heart. He had forgotten his disappointment over not getting to marry the princess and had married the nice swamp monster next door. They had thirty-seven children, eighty-nine grandchildren, and a pet fish named Ralph.

When the swamp monster heard the prince, he rose up through the mud, ran to the castle, picked up the prince, the princess, and the prince's horse, and carried them out of the kingdom.

As soon as they reached the next kingdom, the sun came up. The princess awoke, saw the purple prince, and said, "We were made for each other."

After they thanked the swamp monster, they got married and lived happily ever after.

From then on, every summer the prince and the princess went on vacation to the castle and the swamp monster helped them take sleepers from the castle back with them. Eventually everybody who had fallen asleep because of the spell woke up.

"Those were very good stories," said Monster Goose. "And the stew in the stew pot is ready to eat."

"And I'm ready to eat it," said Zazu.

So Zazu, Moe, Goria, Hexter, and Zack ate stew with Monster Goose. And not one of them cared that it was raining outside because they were all inside.

Joey tried to take in what the Sandman had been saying. "Do you mean you sprinkle sleeping sand on every child in the world?"

"Every child, every night, no exceptions," came the reply.

Joey had so many questions he hardly knew where to begin. But one question came first. "Do you know what happened to the Redd Rocket when I fell? I guess it's gone for good."

"Not to worry, Joey, I caught it in one of my nets. I'll see that you get it back. It's amazing the things I've caught in those shooting star nets over the years. I've made a sort of hobby collecting the stuff. Back home in my windmill I've got a big trunk that's chock full of the most extraordinary things, everything from a polka dot walrus to a one-handed pocket watch. You name it, I've got it."

"Now then," he said, looking out over the bow of the ship, "if my charts are right we should be coming to the spot."

The ship slowed to a stop. Reaching over the side, the old man hoisted up a large golden star that had been hanging from the rail. Across it was the name Kate.

Holding the star out over the side of the ship, the Sandman asked, "Does that look straight, Joey?"

"Yes. I think so."

The Sandman closed his eyes and began to speak:
>"Through stardust and comets
>and wind and bad weather,
>may this star that I hang in the sky
>stay forever!"

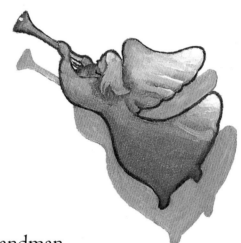

He pulled his hands away. The star floated in place.

"Wow!" said Joey. "How did you do that?"

"Well, let's just say it takes a lot of practice," said the Sandman.

"But why do you put stars in the sky? Aren't there enough already?"

"Every time a child is born I make a new star and hang it in the sky above the town where they were born. Kate was born down there. This is her star.

"Now off we go, no time to waste if we're going to get you home by morning."

May this star that I hang in the sky stay forever

"Where will you go after you take me home?" Joey asked.

"Across the sea and back to my windmill," the Sandman replied. "I need a few winks of sleep myself. Work starts at sunrise."

"But I thought the Sandman only worked at night."

"That's what a lot of people think. People imagine that I just drift about all night sprinkling a bit of sand here and there. Let me tell you it's hard work," said the Sandman. "Just for instance, where do you think the sleeping sand comes from?"

"Well, I never thought . . ." Joey started.

"I'll tell you where," the Sandman continued. "Every morning I sail into the sky and harvest the shooting stars that I've caught in my nets—along with any stray little boys that I happen to find, of course."

24

"Then I take the stars back to the windmill and grind them into fine sleeping sand. That's where it comes from."

"What about the new stars? How do you make those?" asked Joey.

The Sandman was delighted that Joey was so interested in his work. He didn't often get a chance to talk to anyone about it.

"Some of the sand I load onto the ship for sleeping, and some I use to make new stars. I melt the sand in the furnace and pour it into a mold. When it cools, a new star is born. And when a new child is born, I engrave their name on it and hang it in the sky."

*I melt the sand
in the furnace*

Joey looked out at the night sky twinkling with stars and moons as they sailed along. "There are so many stars up here. How do you keep track of them all?"

"With telescopes, charts, and star maps that I keep in the dome of the windmill," the Sandman answered. "I have maps here on board as well, and a log book, too. I write down the names and positions of all the stars on the maps and in the book."

"But some of the stars have numbers," said Joey.

"Those are my navigating stars. At night they help me to find my way around up here. Sort of like street signs and house numbers, if you know what I mean."

Joey nodded.

"Aha!" announced the Sandman. "Off the starboard bow. Star Number 6. That means we're right above your town, Joey. We'll have you home in no time at all."

I write down the
names and positions
of all the stars

Is there a star up here for me?

Joey wasn't quite sure he wanted to go home yet. He was having a fine time, and he didn't want it to end.

He looked down over the side of the ship. He could just make out the rooftops of his town far below as the dawn began to break.

Turning back to the Sandman, he asked, "Is there a star up here for me?" The old man knelt on one knee beside Joey and pointed into the sky. "Right out there."

The boy searched the sky. "Hey, there it is. Right there," he hollered. "It has my name on it and everything!" Then he paused. "How long will it stay up there?"

The Sandman spoke softly. "Through stardust and comets and wind and bad weather, a star that I place in the sky stays forever."

The ship settled like a giant beanbag

The ship settled like a giant beanbag onto the roof of Joey's house in the early light of dawn.

"Here we are, my boy. Safe and sound and right on time."

Joey looked around the ship trying to take it all in so he wouldn't forget this night. Then he looked at the Sandman. "Will I ever see you again?" he asked.

"I'll be by to see you tonight, as always."

"Well, okay," said Joey. "Good-bye for now, and thanks for everything."

Joey paused. "Oh . . . ah, just one more question. How come I'm not sleepy from being on a ship full of sleeping sand?"

The Sandman placed his hand on the boy's shoulder. "Just open your eyes and everything will become clear."

Joey's eyes slowly opened

Joey's eyes slowly opened. He sat up to find himself at home in his bed. Morning light streamed in through the bedroom window. He rubbed his eyes.

"I guess I must have been dreaming," he thought. "I guess there's nothing to tell Henry. But it all seemed so real."

Just then a ray of sun flashed into the corner of the room, lighting up his toybox.

"I knew it!" cried Joey.

There on his toy chest sat the Redd Rocket. It was fully rigged, with a sail, a balloon, and everything. Just like the night before. Just like it was when he'd sailed with the Sandman.

"He said he'd bring it back!

"Henry just won't believe this. He won't believe a word of it."

Joey paused for a minute. A smile came over his face.

"Maybe I won't tell him."

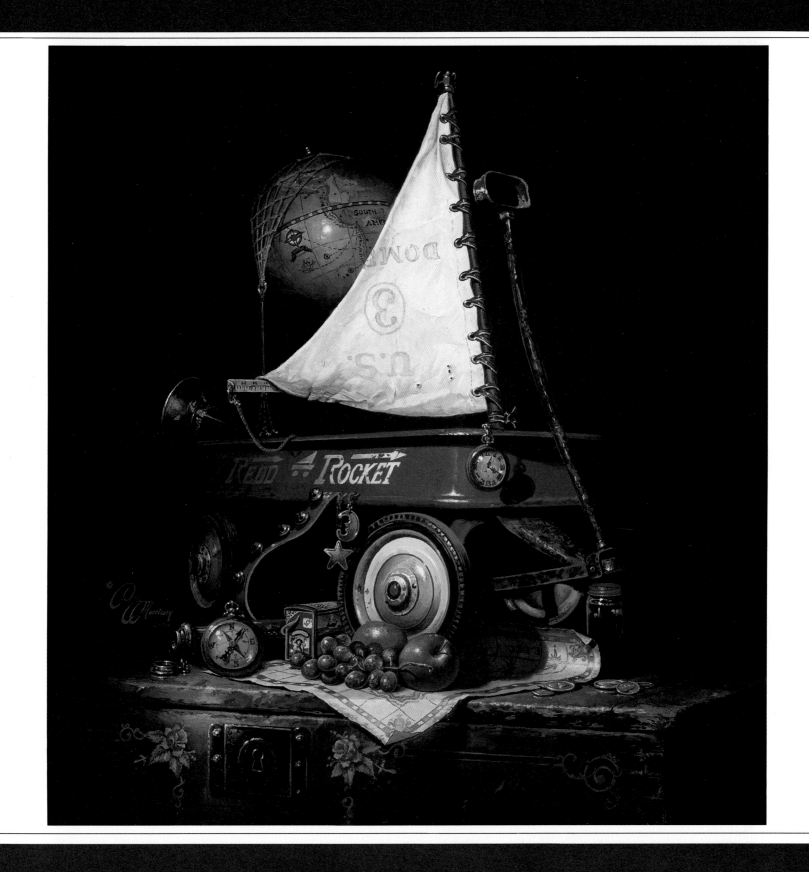

Editor: Robert Morton
Designer: Liz Trovato
Library of Congress Catalog Card Number:
ISBN 0–8109–3848–0

Published in 1994 by Harry N. Abrams, Incorporated, New York
A Times Mirror Company
in association with Mill Pond Press, Inc.,
Venice, Florida, publisher of
Dean Morrissey's limited edition art prints

Index to Artwork

CAROLINA BEACH
ML   9/06

MILITARY MACHINES

ARMORED VEHICLES

By Drew Nelson

Gareth Stevens
Publishing

Please visit our website, www.garethstevens.com. For a free color catalog of all our high-quality books, call toll free 1-800-542-2595 or fax 1-877-542-2596.

Library of Congress Cataloging-in-Publication Data

Nelson, Drew, 1986-
  Armored vehicles / Drew Nelson.
      p. cm. — (Military machines)
  Includes index.
ISBN 978-1-4339-8453-2 (pbk.)
ISBN 978-1-4339-8454-9 (6-pack)
ISBN 978-1-4339-8452-5 (library binding)
1. Armored vehicles, Military—Juvenile literature. 2. Armored vehicles, Military—History—Juvenile literature. I. Title.
 UG446.5.N418 2013
 623.74'75—dc23

                                         2012021809

First Edition

Published in 2013 by
Gareth Stevens Publishing
111 East 14th Street, Suite 349
New York, NY 10003

Copyright © 2013 Gareth Stevens Publishing

Designer: Michael J. Flynn
Editor: Kristen Rajczak

Photo credits: Cover, pp. 1, 19 StockTrek/Getty Images; courtesy of US Army: pp. 4 Spc. Micah E. Clare, 22–23 by C. Todd Lopez, 28–29 by Sgt. David Nunn; p. 5 Carsten Koall/Getty Images; pp. 6, 8 Hulton Archive/Getty Images; pp. 6–7 Fox Photos/Hulton Archive/Getty Images; p. 9 mattesimages/Shutterstock.com; pp. 10–11 JeP/Shutterstock.com; pp. 12–13, 27 PhotoQuest/Archive Photos/Getty Images; p. 14 Scott Nelson/Getty Images; p. 14 Hrvoje Polan/AFP/Getty Images; p. 15 Genya Savilov/AFP/Getty Images; p. 17 Paul J. Richards/AFP/Getty Images; p. 18 Stephen Morton/Getty Images; p. 21 Bloomberg/Getty Images; p. 23 http://en.wikipedia.org/wiki/File:British_Mark_IX_Armoured_Personnel_Carrier.jpg; p. 24 http://en.wikipedia.org/wiki/File:M22_Locust_light_tank_at_Bovington.jpg; p. 25 http://en.wikipedia.org/wiki/File:LittleWillie.jpg; p. 26 G. Cigolini/De Agostini Picture Library/Getty Images.

Printed in the United States of America

CPSIA compliance information: Batch #CW13GS: For further information contact Gareth Stevens, New York, New York at 1-800-542-2595.

CONTENTS

Words in the glossary appear in **bold** type the first time they are used in the text.

WHAT ARE ARMORED VEHICLES?

The US military uses many different kinds of machines to help complete their **missions** around the world. These machines include armored **vehicles**, submarines, spy planes, fighter jets, and helicopters. All these machines help people in the military fight enemies, rescue those in need, and collect **information**.

Armored vehicles are an important part of US military operations.

385 MP

MP310

4

Armored vehicles have heavy protective shells to keep safe the people or supplies they're carrying. Tanks are some of the best-known armored vehicles—and for good reason. These military machines can be huge! But since World War I, other armored vehicles, such as armored cars and **personnel** carriers, have also been used to protect soldiers and citizens alike.

Famous Armored Vehicles

There are a few nonmilitary armored vehicles that have become well known around the world. One is the "Popemobile," the armored car the leader of the Catholic Church rides in. Another is the limousine of the president of the United States, which is armor plated and protected by the Secret Service.

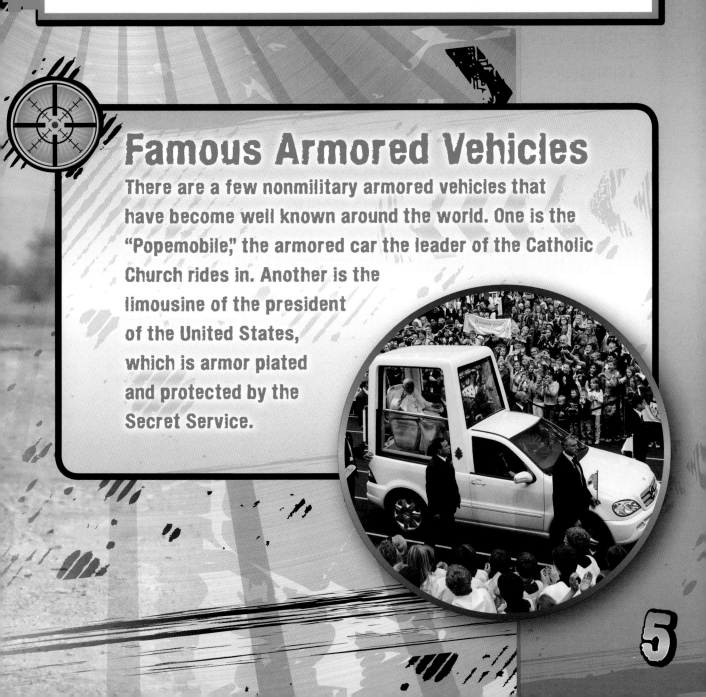

HISTORY OF ARMORED VEHICLES

You may picture recently invented tanks and trucks when you think of armored vehicles. But the first plan for an armored vehicle was drawn in 1485! Famous Italian inventor and artist Leonardo da Vinci made drawings for an armored war vehicle armed with cannons. It turned out his plan wouldn't work the way he had imagined it, though.

The first armored vehicles to be produced were armored cars made by Rolls-Royce. Based on the company's Silver Ghost model, these heavily armored cars with gun **turrets** were used in World War I, starting in August 1914. They were part of the Royal Naval Air Service in Great Britain.

Silver Ghost

Lawrence of Arabia

Colonel T. E. Lawrence, famously known as Lawrence of Arabia, used nine Rolls-Royce armored cars for his missions in the Middle East. They were used for fighting in difficult desert conditions. Lawrence once stated that the cars were "more valuable than rubies."

The British army used armored cars like this one in the 1930s.

ARMORED VEHICLES IN WWI

More types of armored vehicles were **developed** for World War I. British military leader Winston Churchill supported ideas for vehicles with armor, machine guns, tracks, and **artillery**. The British called these machines "water tanks" to keep what they really were a secret. They were first used on September 15, 1916, at the Battle of the Somme in France.

Though early tanks were effective at scattering German troops, they often broke down or had trouble communicating with Allied forces during battles.

By 1918, the Allied armies of Britain, France, and the United States had more than 500 tanks to fight their World War I enemies, the Central powers, which included Bulgaria, and the German, Turkish, and Austro-Hungarian empires. These early armored vehicles helped the Allies score major victories.

Tracks or treads are large bands moved by wheels that are often seen on tanks, bulldozers, and other vehicles used for travel over rough ground.

Plan 1919

Before the Germans **surrendered** to the Allies, a British army officer named John Frederick Charles Fuller came up with a plan. He wanted to attack the Germans with more than 5,000 tanks in an attempt to end the war. The war ended before his "Plan 1919" could be used.

9

INTERWAR PERIOD

Between World War I and World War II, the United States started to develop more armored vehicles, such as advanced armored cars. These included scout cars, which were used to collect information on enemy movements and as a replacement for **cavalry**, and the M3 Armored Half-Track.

Half-tracks like the M3 are useful to the military because they can run on streets like a car but cover many **terrains** like a tank.

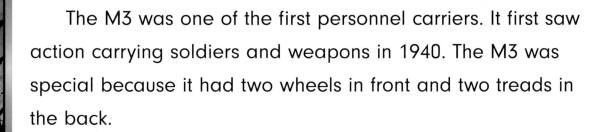

The M3 was one of the first personnel carriers. It first saw action carrying soldiers and weapons in 1940. The M3 was special because it had two wheels in front and two treads in the back.

Not So Fast or Furious

While early scout cars and the M3 Armored Half-Track were groundbreaking for their time, they couldn't move nearly as fast as modern cars. The top speed for the M3 was only 45 miles (72 km) per hour!

TANKS OF WWII

In the early years of World War II, the German military won many victories because of its use of armored vehicles. In 1941, the Germans had great success against Russian forces with new movements and plans using tanks. It showed they had changed their approach to fighting on land after World War I.

In response to this, the United States started building more and more tanks. In 1943, the army had 16 armored divisions and 65 tank battalions. By 1945, the United States had produced more than 90,000 tanks! The US Army had better firepower and movement ability than ever before. Using these armored vehicles, the US military helped win the war.

Tank Masters

Two famous German tank commanders of World War II were Generals Heinz Guderian and Erwin Rommel. General Guderian was a commander of the Panzer forces, the name for the best-known kind of German tanks. General Rommel became known as the "Desert Fox" following his battles in North Africa.

The German military started making Panzers, shown here, during the 1930s. Six models of the tank were made before the end of World War II.

US ARMORED VEHICLES AFTER WWII

Even though tanks helped the United States and its allies win World War II, they weren't always useful in later wars and conflicts. During the Korean War, US armored vehicles couldn't move around the rough terrain and mountains of Korea well and had to stay on roads. The army also had problems fighting against the bigger, newer tanks of the Soviet Union because it was still using tanks from World War II.

M1A1 Abrams

During the Cold War, the United States worked on many new tank ideas. Larger armored vehicles as advanced as other countries' vehicles were added to US forces around this time.

Soviet T-34

The Massive M1

One of the large Cold War—era tanks that the United States made in the 1980s was the M1 Abrams. This vehicle had almost 18 inches (46 cm) of armor protecting the crew inside. Later models had more than 30 inches (76 cm) of armor!

THE ARMOR

Each kind of armored vehicle has a job to do. The type and amount of armor it has reflect these different tasks. Vehicles that need to move quickly in and out of places have to be light and fast, so they have less armor. Vehicles that are made to attack enemy forces or keep the people inside safe have heavier armor, which makes them weigh more and move more slowly.

Since tanks encounter the most weapons, they have the most armor, usually made out of metal and ceramic. Armored cars and recovery vehicles have less armor, sometimes made of special plastics.

Just How Heavy Can Armor Be?

The vehicles that are built to take the most damage, main battle tanks, also have the heaviest and toughest armor. They can weigh up to 70 tons (64 metric tons). All that weight is worth it, though—some of these tanks are built to withstand nuclear explosions!

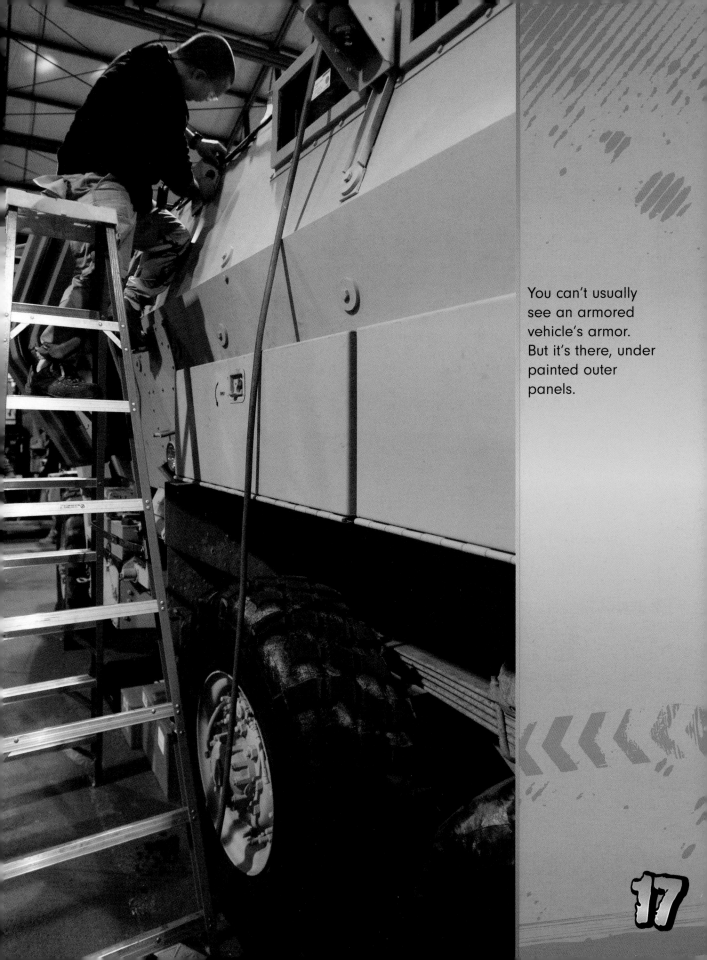

You can't usually
see an armored
vehicle's armor.
But it's there, under
painted outer
panels.

THE WEAPONS

Armored vehicles can be outfitted with many different kinds of weapons to protect the soldiers in the vehicle and fight enemies. Lighter vehicles that move faster, such as armored cars, have fewer weapons. Armored personnel carriers act primarily as a way to bring soldiers to and from the battlefield, so they don't have many weapons. Light-armored vehicles have machine guns mounted on them.

Bigger and more heavily armored vehicles, like tanks and **infantry** fighting vehicles, have more and deadlier weapons. These may include machine guns, cannons, missiles, 120- or 125-millimeter guns, or even grenade launchers!

A US Army soldier aims a machine gun from the top of an armored truck.

Main battle tanks like this one offer firepower as well as protection for soldiers.

A Tank's Secret Weapons

Many tanks are outfitted with more than just their heavy armor, weapons, and the soldiers inside. Some tanks have smoke generators that spew out smoke to make it hard for enemies to detect them. Many also have computerized fire-control systems that can fire weapons without a soldier pulling the trigger.

TYPES OF MILITARY ARMORED VEHICLES

While the first armored cars were used only by the military, today, some car companies make them for anyone who can afford them. One company from Latvia even sells a gold-plated armored car!

The main armored vehicles used for fighting are called armored fighting vehicles, or AFVs. The main battle tank (MBT) is the most powerful and heavily armored AFV. In 2012, the Japanese began using the TK-X MBT, a new AFV model that's not only lighter, but also able to "lean" in any direction during battle! Today, the United States still commonly uses the Abrams tank, though it has been updated many times since the 1980s.

Big Money

Most of the time, the military uses vehicles that are made with their armor already on. Sometimes, though, people take other vehicles and have armor added to them to make them safer. Getting armor put on a vehicle can cost a lot of money—sometimes even up to $1 million!

Putting armor on a vehicle is like putting together a puzzle piece by piece.

21

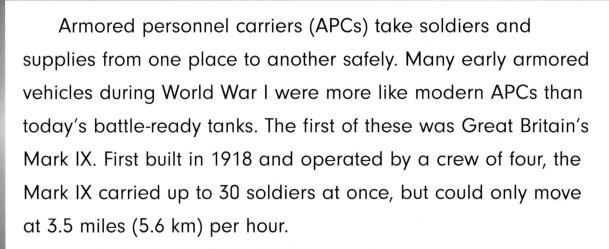

Armored personnel carriers (APCs) take soldiers and supplies from one place to another safely. Many early armored vehicles during World War I were more like modern APCs than today's battle-ready tanks. The first of these was Great Britain's Mark IX. First built in 1918 and operated by a crew of four, the Mark IX carried up to 30 soldiers at once, but could only move at 3.5 miles (5.6 km) per hour.

Other Stryker models, such as the one pictured here, are used for scouting missions.

The M1126 Stryker Infantry Carrier Vehicle is a modern APC made by the United States. It can carry nine soldiers, and its top speed is more than 60 miles (97 km) per hour!

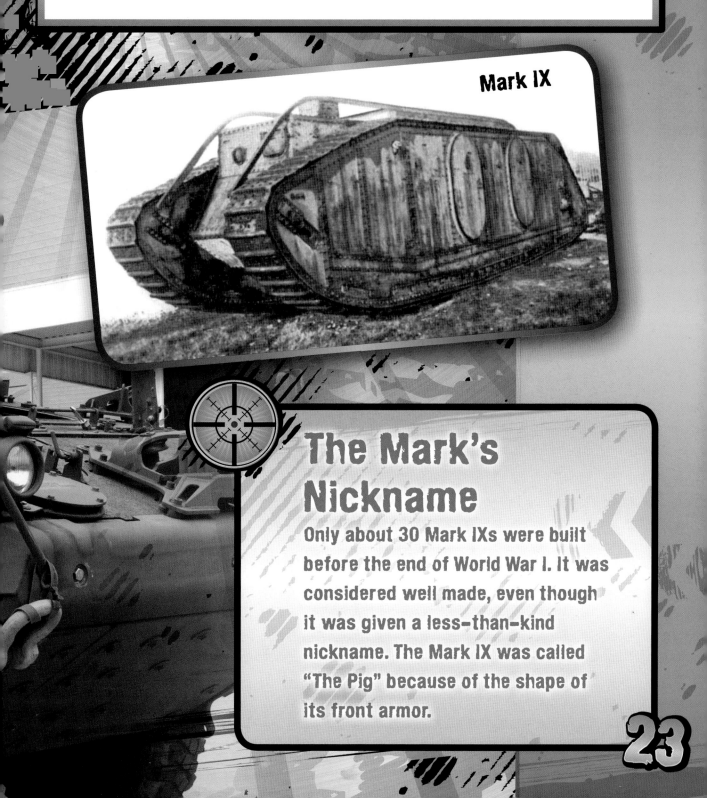

Mark IX

The Mark's Nickname

Only about 30 Mark IXs were built before the end of World War I. It was considered well made, even though it was given a less-than-kind nickname. The Mark IX was called "The Pig" because of the shape of its front armor.

The main job of an infantry fighting vehicle (IFV) is moving with ground forces to fight enemies. It supports individual soldiers or small groups of soldiers on the battlefield, so it must be smaller and faster than tanks.

One cool kind of IFV was the M22 Locust. These light, small vehicles could be dropped onto battlefields from airplanes! Each could only fit three soldiers, but once on the ground, the Locust could fight and travel about 135 miles (217 km). The Locusts were first built in 1943 by the United States during World War II, but few saw **combat**.

This M22 Locust can be seen at a museum as part of collection of other historical tanks.

Little Willie

Little Willie

One of the first-ever armored fighting vehicles that moved on tracks was called "Little Willie." The British built it in 1915 based on the idea of farm tractors. While this first tank wasn't suitable for the rough battlefields of World War I, "Little Willie" led to the development of modern AFVs.

The Greyhound only had light armor, and early models were often damaged by landmines that hit their less-protected underside.

Armored **reconnaissance** vehicles (ARVs) go into enemy territory ahead of the rest of the ground army to collect information on enemy forces, positions, and terrain. One important part of victory during World War II was the development of a series of ARVs known as scout cars. The M8 Greyhound was the most well known of these.

Thousands of M8 Greyhounds were built during World War II. They had six tires that helped them move quickly through many terrains. The M8 had headlights and rearview mirrors to help soldiers drive it, just like a modern car.

The M4 Sherman

The most well-known tank used by the United States during World War II was the M4 Sherman. This medium-sized tank was named for a Civil War general and was the first AFV that could compete with the tanks built by the Germans.

Sherman tanks were first used for combat in 1942.

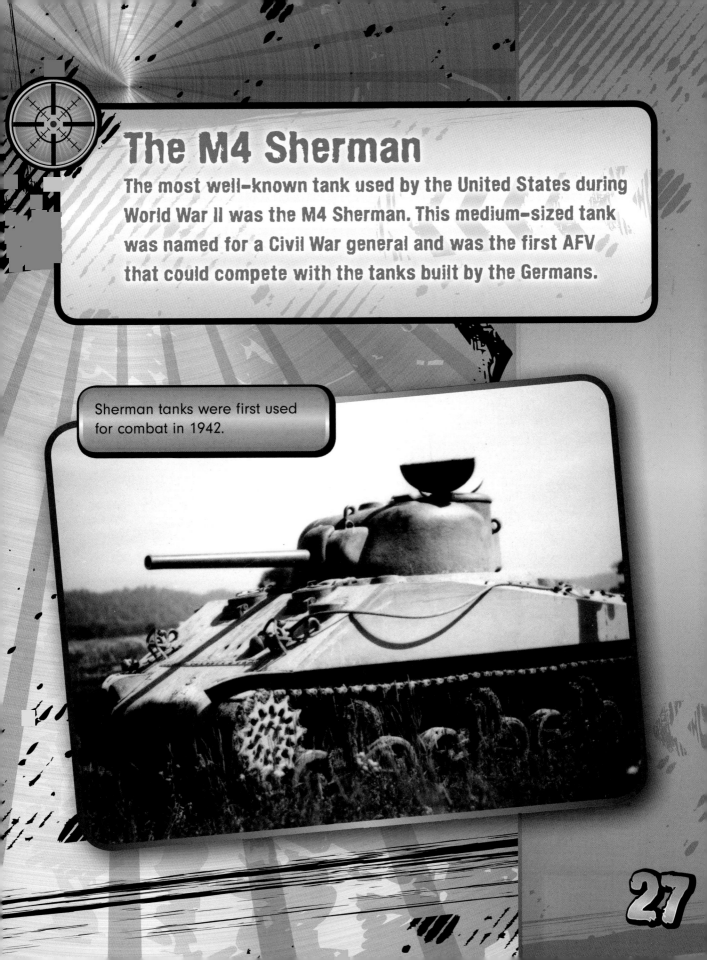

THE FUTURE OF ARMORED VEHICLES

In modern warfare, land battles are fought very differently from how they were fought during the world wars. There are even some people who say tanks are no longer effective on the battlefield. This could be because of weapons advances, including armor-piercing weapons and "smart" missiles that can be controlled from far away with computers.

US forces have brought more than 1,000 tanks to the Middle East since invading Iraq in 2003.

However, better, more effective tanks—with lighter armor and their own "smart" weapons—are being built all over the world. As long as the US military sends soldiers into battle, it will need tanks and other armored vehicles to help protect them.

Targeting Tanks

The battlefields of the US invasion of Iraq weren't always clear. Enemies didn't move in clear lines or as forces, making it harder to use tanks in combat. Often, a tank's heavy armor is in the front. A sneak attack from the rear by a single soldier could really damage even big tanks like the Abrams.

GLOSSARY

artillery: large guns that shoot shells, bullets, or missiles

cavalry: members of the army that ride horses

combat: armed fighting between opposing forces

develop: to grow and change

infantry: soldiers trained to fight on foot

information: knowledge obtained from study or observation

mission: a task or job a group must perform

personnel: a group of people who work at a place

reconnaissance: the exploration of a place to collect information

surrender: to give up

terrain: the type of land in an area

turret: an armored structure on top of a tank that holds a gun and can be moved side to side or in a circle

vehicle: an object used for carrying or transporting people or goods, such as a car, truck, or airplane

FOR MORE INFORMATION

Books

Peppas, Lynn. *Powerful Armored Vehicles.* New York, NY: Crabtree Publishing, 2012.

Shank, Carol. *U.S. Military Assault Vehicles.* North Mankato, MN: Capstone Press, 2013.

Von Finn, Denny. *Abrams Tanks.* Minneapolis, MN: Bellwether Media, 2013.

Websites

Military Factory
www.militaryfactory.com
Check out historical weapons and vehicles using this military reference.

US Army Homepage
www.army.mil
Use the US Army website to find out more information about wheeled and tracked military vehicles.

INDEX